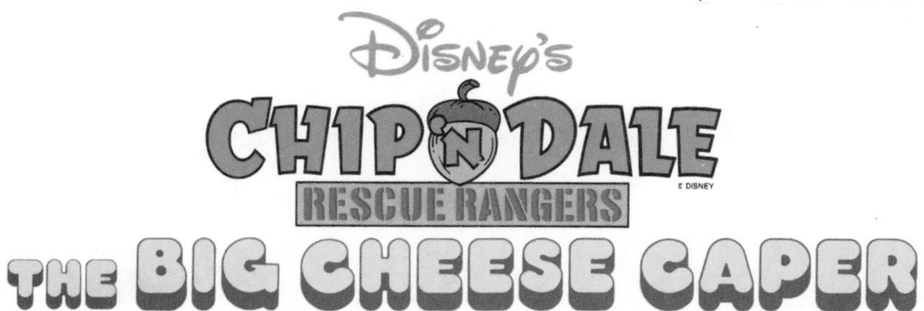

By Deborah Kovacs
Illustrated by Darrell Baker

A GOLDEN BOOK • NEW YORK
Western Publishing Company, Inc., Racine, Wisconsin 53404

Library of Congress Catalog Card Number: 91-70456 ISBN: 0-307-00646-8
MCMXCII

Chip and Dale and the Rescue Rangers were taking an overnight train ride to the World Cheese Festival. The train was very crowded. Chip and Dale had never seen so many mice in one place at the same time.

Inside the train, Chip and Dale's friend Gadget held up a shiny metal tool. "I'm going to show this drill that I made, at the festival," Gadget said. "It's for putting holes in Swiss cheese."

"Time to practice for the yodeling contest," said Monterey Jack, opening his mouth wide. "YODELAY-HEE-HOOOOOO!"

None of them noticed the sly lizard who stared at Gadget's Swiss cheese drill and then slinked away.

Beside the Rescue Rangers sat a mouse with his nose buried in a big book, the *Encyclopedia of Cheese, Volume 1*. Dale nudged Chip. "Can you imagine reading a book like that?" he whispered loudly.

"This is a most interesting book," the mouse said. "I wrote it. I'm Professor Girvin Gouda, and I'm going to win the Biggest Cheese in the World Contest." He handed the book to Chip. "Why don't you read this? If you like it, I'll send you the other nineteen volumes."

Chip swallowed hard and smiled.

"Would you like to see the cheese I am entering in the contest?" Professor Gouda continued.

The Rescue Rangers followed the professor to the last car of the train. It was bright pink on the outside, and on the inside it was filled with Professor Gouda's cheese—a two-thousand-pound white cheddar.

"Wow!" said Gadget.

"It *is* rather special, isn't it?" said the professor, beaming.

"What a cheese!" said Dale as they went back to their seats.

"What a smell!" said Chip, sniffing the air. "Isn't that—"

"Happy Tom Cat Food!" said all the Rescue Rangers at once. Following their noses, the Rescue Rangers soon came to the closed door of a train compartment. Through the frosted glass, they could see the shape of their archenemy—Fat Cat.

"What is *he* doing here?" said Dale.

"I don't know, but I wish we could hear what he's saying!" said Chip.

Inside the compartment, Fat Cat was talking to his evil crew. "Tonight we will steal Professor Gouda's cheese and disguise it so that nobody will recognize it," he said. "Then we'll win first prize for the biggest cheese in the world!"

"What's the prize, boss?" asked a lizard.

"It's a free trip to Switzerland," said Fat Cat, grinning wickedly. "I deserve a nice vacation, don't you think, my little helpers?"

"Yes, boss!" they all said at the same time.

“We’ve got to find out what Fat Cat is up to,” Chip told Dale. “I don’t trust him as far as I could throw him.”

“And that’s not very far,” said Dale.

That night the Rescue Rangers staked out Fat Cat’s train compartment, waiting to see what he would do next. But nothing happened. Finally they went to bed.

At dawn, Professor Gouda shook Chip and Dale awake.

"My CHEESE!" he wailed. "It's GONE!"

They all raced to the rear of the train. Sure enough, the pink train car full of cheese was gone. "Fat Cat!" said Chip and Dale. They ran to Fat Cat's compartment, but it was empty.

Gadget screamed, “My Swiss cheese drill! It’s GONE!”

“There must be some connection,” said Chip.

“I think the connection is a big, nasty cat,” said Dale.

“Zipper!” called Chip. “Find Fat Cat!” The little fly could find anything—and fast. Zipper disappeared and returned, almost instantly, pointing south.

As the train pulled into a station, Dale spotted a little handcar. "We can use it to find Fat Cat," he said. Chip slipped on a backpack, and the chipmunks scrambled onto the handcar. They pumped the handle with all their might.

Soon they saw the pink train car, standing still. It was hooked up to a purple engine with the words FAT CAT EXPRESS painted on the side.

Inside the train car, Chip and Dale could see Fat Cat grinning as he watched one of his rats use Gadget's drill on Professor Gouda's cheese.

"That sneaky feline," said Chip. "He thinks he can disguise the cheddar as Swiss cheese! He'll never get away with this!"

"What are we going to do?" asked Dale.

"I have a plan," said Chip.

Meanwhile, the train full of mice had arrived at the World Cheese Festival. Professor Gouda was very worried about his cheese. Gadget and Monterey Jack tried to cheer him up.

"Now, now, Professor," said Monterey Jack. "Chip and Dale will find your cheese. They *never* mess up. Well, almost never."

“Why don’t we look around at the festival,” said Gadget. “They’ll be here soon.”

“I hope so,” said Professor Gouda miserably.

Gadget and Professor Gouda watched a big group of mice compete in the mozzarella cheese pull. Monterey Jack won first prize in the yodeling contest. But there was still no sign of the pink train car. “It’s almost time for the judging,” said Professor Gouda, shaking his head.

SWAMP
LIFE

Meanwhile, on the pink-and-purple train, Chip and Dale climbed up near the engine and saw their old friend Sewer Al, reading an old copy of *Swamp Life* magazine. Sewer Al was always reading.

"Hi, there," said Chip.

"What?" gasped the alligator, so surprised that he fell off his motorman's chair.

"Sewer Al," said Chip, talking fast, "let's make a deal. If you help us get Fat Cat and his crew off the train, I'll *give* you this wonderful book." From his backpack he pulled out the first volume of the *Encyclopedia of Cheese*. "Not only that," Chip added. "There are nineteen more volumes in this set. I'll give you *all* of them."

"What a deal!" said Sewer Al.

Their friend hopped off the train and called to Fat Cat. "Hey, Cat! Come down here. I think I found a whole case of tuna fish!"

"Really?" said Fat Cat. He and his mangy crew jumped down off the train.

Chip and Dale started the engine. The train rolled away, leaving Fat Cat shaking his fist beside the railroad track.

Back at the festival, Professor Gouda watched sadly as a medium-sized Limburger was about to be named the Biggest Cheese in the World. "If only my cheese were here," he said with a sigh.

All of a sudden Professor Gouda heard, "WHOO-WHOO!"

"It's the train!" he shouted. He grabbed two of the judges and explained what had happened to his cheese. "Come with me!" he said. The judges followed him to the train.

"What a cheese!" said one.

"You win first prize!" said another.

"Hurray!" cried Professor Gouda and the Rescue Rangers.

A few weeks later the Rescue Rangers struggled to keep up with Professor Gouda as he scrambled up a huge, snowy mountain.

"It sure was nice of you to take us with you to Switzerland!" shouted Chip.

"I'd never have won this free trip if it weren't for you," said Professor Gouda. "You Rescue Rangers are wonderful!"

"Cheese! It was nothing!" said Dale.